MY FRIEND THE DOCTOR

by JOANNA COLE

illustrated by MAXIE CHAMBLISS

HarperCollinsPublishers

To Annabelle Pearl Helms

—J.C.

For letting the author sit in on checkups, heartfelt thanks go to Dr. Barry Keller;
nurse Sue Markowski; Abby Giansiracusa and her father, Paul; and Abigail and
Paul Saunders and their mother, Karen. It was fun!

My Friend the Doctor

Text copyright © 2005 by Joanna Cole

Illustrations copyright © 2005 by Maxie Chambliss

Library of Congress Cataloging-in-Publication Data

Cole, Joanna.

  My friend the doctor / by Joanna Cole ; illustrated by Maxie Chambliss.—1st ed.   p.   cm.

  Summary: Describes Hannah's visit to the doctor's office for a routine examination.

ISBN 0-06-050500-1

  [1. Physicians—Fiction.   2. Health—Fiction.   3. Medical care—Fiction.]   I. Chambliss, Maxie, ill.   II. Title.

PZ7.C67346Mye   2005   2004014797

[E]—dc22

Typography by Amelia Anderson   1   2   3   4   5   6   7   8   9   10   ❖   First Edition

The first time Hannah went to her doctor, she was a brand-new baby.

Welcome, Hannah!

Then Hannah grew and grew.
Now she's big, just like you!

Hannah likes to go for a checkup.
First she plays with the toys
in the waiting room.
Do you like toys, too?

Then Nurse Marks weighs Hannah on a big scale . . .

and sees how tall she is.

Dr. Kelly comes in.
He asks Hannah's mommy,
"How has Hannah been?"
Mommy says, "Fine and healthy!"

The doctor's checkup will help *keep* Hannah healthy.

First Dr. Kelly uses his stethoscope to listen to Hannah's heart.

Hannah hears Dr. Kelly's heart, too.

Now Dr. Kelly uses a light
to check Hannah's mouth . . .

and her eyes . . .

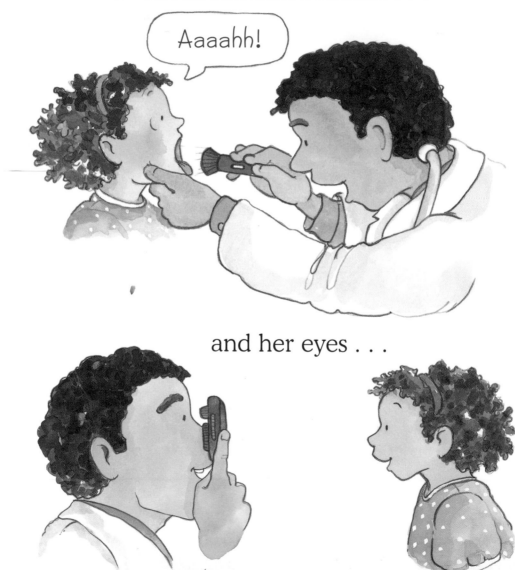

and her ears.

Dr. Kelly feels Hannah's belly to make sure her insides are healthy.

He makes sure her knee jerks when he taps it with a little hammer.

"Can you touch your toes?"
asks Dr. Kelly.

"Will you walk to the
door and back again?"

Dr. Kelly watches her walk.
"Everything is fine," he says.
"Hannah is a healthy girl!"

Nurse Marks gives Hannah a shot to help her stay healthy.

It hurts for a second, but Mommy squeezes Hannah's hand and shows her something funny. Then Hannah doesn't feel the shot so much.

Look at that silly pig!

Nurse Marks lets Hannah
pick out a sticker.
Which one would you pick?

Hannah says thank you and good-bye.
She likes her doctor and nurse.
It was a good checkup!

Note to Parents

Preparing Children for Checkups

When to get ready: Tell your child about the upcoming visit the day before, or even the day of, the visit. Too long a lead time may increase anxiety.

Tell what to expect: Read a book like this one with your child.

Play it out: Encourage your child to examine a doll or stuffed animal with a toy doctor's kit.

Take a special toy: Let your child choose a toy or special blanket to take along. Some doctors will even "examine" a doll or stuffed animal.

Let your child be in control: Encourage your child to help the nurse and doctor by staying still. Some children may enjoy making a drawing or other gift for the doctor and nurse.

Emphasize the fun parts: Mention that there are toys and books in the waiting room, and that the doctor and nurse are nice.

Tell the truth about the difficult parts: If a shot is expected, say that it will hurt but only for a few seconds.

Plan for a distraction: Bring along bubbles to blow just as the shot goes in; pull out a photograph to look at; make a funny face or noise; sing a song; even just squeeze your child's hand or tap a different part of her body.

Choose a doctor who is friendly to children: If the doctor you are seeing seems distant or unsympathetic, don't be afraid to find a new one. Ask friends and other doctors for recommendations.

After the visit: Find something to praise. Emphasize the positives and ignore the negatives. For example, tell your child, "I liked the way you said thank you," but ignore the fact that he wiggled on the table. Then, just before the next visit, remind him to help by staying still.